Hava Deevon

Barefoot in the Sand

Illustrated by Rotem Teplow
Translated by Gilah Kahn-Hoffman

First published in the UK in 2023 by Green Bean Books

c/o Pen & Sword Books Ltd

47 Church Street, Barnsley, South Yorkshire, S70 2AS

www.greenbeanbooks.com

Barefoot in the Sand was first published by Kinneret, Zmora-Bitan, Dvir in 2019 as the result of the initiative of Keren Grinspoon's Sifriyat Pijama program in Israel.

Green Bean paperback edition: 978-1-78438-926-0

Harold Grinspoon Foundation edition: 978-180-500-013-6

Designed by Gilad Visotsky

Edited by Lisa Silverman and Rachael Stein

Production by Hugh Allan

Printed in China by Leo Paper Products Ltd

1023/B2360/A6

When Saul was just a boy, he dreamed of living in a place called *Eretz Yisrael* — the land of Israel.

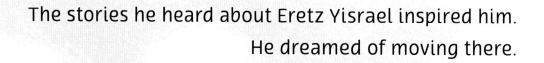

The stories he heard about Eretz Yisrael inspired him.
He dreamed of moving there.

But he wasn't old enough yet, so instead he imagined what it would be like to wander through grassy fields, climb rocky hills, and walk barefoot on warm, golden sand.

Saul grew older. At his Jewish school in Romania, he learned all about the land of Israel. He wanted more than anything to go there. But he still wasn't old enough, so he continued to wait and dream.

He dreamed about digging deep into the soil to plant young saplings that, with time and patience, would grow into strong trees full of apples and figs.

When he was finally old enough, Saul came up with a plan. In those days, people traveled long distances by train and boat. So he would take a train to a port on the coast and board a boat to cross the Mediterranean Sea. He would wear his shoes, of course, because it was cold in his country. But when he arrived in Eretz Yisrael, he would buy sandals for the hot summer days and a hat to protect him from the blazing sun.

Days and nights passed, and years went by. Eventually, the day came for Saul to make his journey.

After weeks at sea, he caught his first glimpse of Tel Aviv. His dream had finally come true — he had reached the land of Israel!

He stepped off the boat onto dry land. The sun beat down on him, and he laughed, giddy with joy.

He remembered how he had imagined Eretz Yisrael when he was just a boy. He looked down at his heavy boots and kicked them off. He wanted to feel the soft sand between his toes.

Hallelujah!

His next thought was to say the Hallel prayer, a Jewish psalm of praise and thanks. "When the Jews left Egypt — a place so strange to Jacob and all his descendants — the Land of Israel became their haven and their home."

In those days, Tel Aviv was a small city surrounded by magnificent golden sand dunes. Saul left his shoes and suitcase with an officer at the port and started to walk.

The sand was pleasant but hot, a little hotter than he had imagined. The shouts of the sailors, the bustle of other passengers, and the cries of seagulls all faded away. It was just Saul and the sand of his dreams.

As he walked along the desert sands, Saul thought he saw a figure approaching. Was he dreaming?

It was hard to see in the blazing sun. But as he continued to walk, Saul realized the figure was a man, and the man was coming closer.

How strange, Saul thought. This other man wasn't carrying a jacket like he was. He wasn't wearing a shirt or suit pants, and he didn't have a sunhat.

Instead, the stranger wore a cotton tunic and a turban on his head. His skin was dark and his hair was long. There was only one thing they had in common: the man coming closer had no shoes. He was barefoot too!

Saul gazed at the stranger in front of him
and didn't know how to greet him.

The man's bare feet reminded Saul of his own journey
and the Hallel prayer. So he raised his voice and sang:
"When the Jews left Egypt..."

WHEN THE JEW
LEFT EGYPT — A PLACE SC
STRANGE TO JACOB AND
ALL HIS DESCENDANTS—

The stranger smiled and replied in song, "a place so strange to Jacob and all his descendants."

"The Land of Israel became their haven," Saul continued.
Then he paused, waiting for the other man to join in, and together they sang, "and their home."

THE LAND OF ISRAEL BECAME THEIR HAVEN AND THEIR HOME.

Then the two men burst out laughing. Why? Because though they were both speaking the same language, their accents were so different!

"Why are you barefoot?" one asked the other.

"Because I've waited so many years to feel the sand of Eretz Israel between my toes," was the answer.

It doesn't matter who asked and who answered. Both men had dreamed of the Land of Israel since they were children. And now here they were, both barefoot, both feeling the sand beneath their feet.

"My name is Saul. I am from the country of Romania,
far north of here. I traveled for many weeks by train and boat."

"My name is Solomon. I am from the country of Yemen, far *south* of here. I rode on a donkey, and I also traveled for a very long time," the stranger replied.

"I crossed the Mediterranean Sea on a big ship," said Saul. And he enthusiastically stretched his arms out wide to show how big the ship was.

"I crossed the mighty desert by donkey and camel",
Solomon answered, also spreading his arms out wide.

They joyfully held each other's hands
and danced the *hora*...

a Jewish man from Arabian lands
with a Jewish man from Europe.

Both barefoot on the hot sand.

Not strangers, but brothers.

Hava Deevon

Barefoot In the Sand

Illustrated by Rotem Teplow

Translated by Gilah Kahn-Hoffman

Green
Bean
Books

www.greenbeanbooks.com